Randolph is mostly
very, very nice.

When Randolph Turned ROTTEN

STINKY,
ROTTEN
INSIDES

by **Charise Mericle Harper**

Alfred A. Knopf — New York

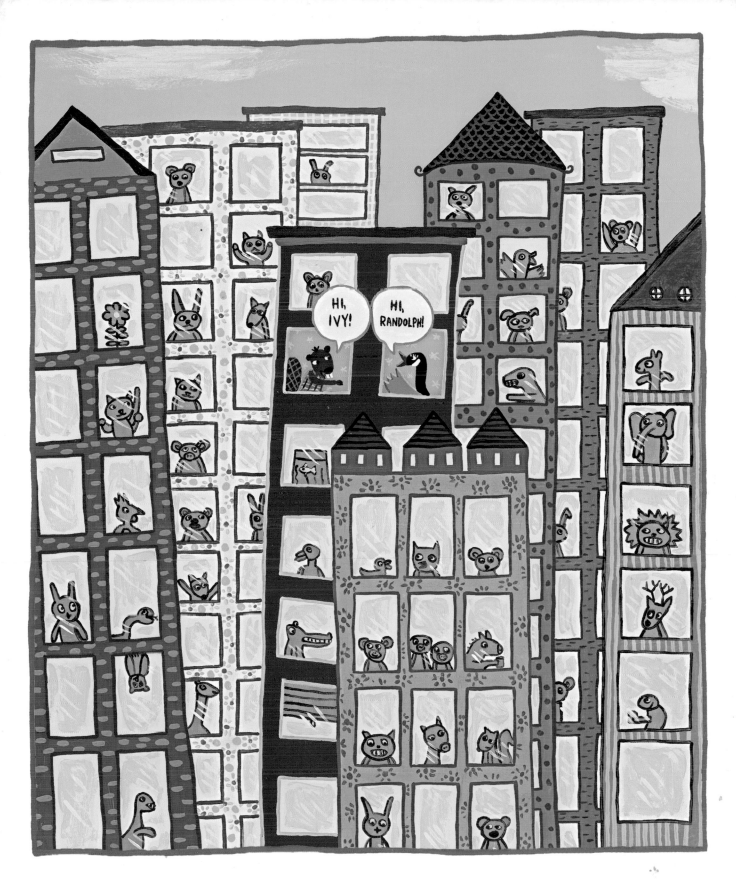

In a big city, in a little apartment, lived two friends.

They liked to eat together,

and play together,

and sit in matching chairs reading their favorite bedtime stories.

One morning, good news arrived,

but not for Randolph.

Ivy was so excited about her invitation, she talked about it . . .

morning,

noon,

and night.

All of Ivy's party talking started to make
Randolph do some wishing.

Most of all, he wished for this:

When Ivy started to pack, Randolph made a new wish . . .

and a plan.

And that's when Randolph's insides changed
from very-best-friend insides

BEST FRIEND RANDOLPH

to horrible, rotten, awful, and icky insides.

NASTY RANDOLPH

But Ivy didn't even notice that her very best friend had changed.

And here's what nasty-on-the-inside Randolph did:

He told his very best friend this:

And this:

And this:

And even this!

Then he finished packing Ivy's suitcase.

The next day was goodbye-to-Ivy day.

STAYING
HOME

GOING ON
A TRIP

Randolph was very pleased with what he had done.

At first, he did all sorts of things he couldn't do when Ivy was around.

He gave the seesaw a nibble.

He shouted out the window.

He stretched out on BOTH bedtime chairs.

But nothing was as much fun without Ivy.

And Randolph started feeling . . . very guilty.

Meanwhile, Ivy had just arrived at Cousin Ava's house.

Everyone came out to meet Ivy.

And then something bad happened.

They were locked out of the house.

Cousin Ava was very sad.

Everyone tried to help.

When Ivy opened her bag, she was very surprised.

It was a wonderful idea.

They followed Ivy's flashing hat to the beach.

At the beach party, they played freeze tag,

invited some new friends to play duck-duck-goose,

and sang "Happy Birthday" under the starry sky.

And even though Ivy realized that
he had been wrong about
the beach bears

and the beach snakes,

she was still glad to have a best friend
like Randolph.

When morning came, Ivy couldn't wait to get home to
tell Randolph what had happened.

Randolph couldn't wait for Ivy to get home so he
could tell her how sorry he was.

The two friends saw each other across the park.

Randolph hugged Ivy extra tight.

And then Ivy showed Randolph his special necklace,

and she told him:

Then, because they were still the very best of friends,
they sat in their matching chairs
to share a bedtime story.

And Randolph knew that his very best friend really did forgive him.

THIS IS A BORZOI BOOK PUBLISHED BY ALFRED A. KNOPF

Copyright © 2007 by Charise Mericle Harper

www.randomhouse.com/kids

Educators and librarians, for a variety of teaching tools, visit us at
www.randomhouse.com/teachers

Library of Congress Cataloging-In-Publication Data
Harper, Charise Mericle.
When Randolph turned rotten / by Charise Mericle Harper. – 1st ed.
p. cm.
SUMMARY: Best friends Randolph, a beaver, and Ivy, a goose, do everything together until Ivy is invited to a
girls-only birthday sleepover party and Randolph, full of bad feelings, tries to spoil her fun.
ISBN 978-0-375-84071-5 (trade) – ISBN 978-0-375 94071-2 (lib. bdg.)
[1. Best friends–Fiction. 2. Friendship–Fiction. 3. Sleepovers–Fiction. 4. Birthdays–Fiction. 5. Behavior–Fiction.
6. Beavers–Fiction. 7. Geese–Fiction.] I. Title.
PZ7.H231325Whe 2007
[E]–dc22
2006030572

The illustrations in this book were created using acrylic on illustration board.

MANUFACTURED IN MALAYSIA
November 2007
10 9 8 7 6 5 4 3 2 1

First Edition